IN CLOSE QUARTERS

QUARTERS

GAY MILE-HIGH CLUB LOVE STORY

ANGUS MacGREGOR

WARNING

This book contains sexually explicit scenes and adult language. It may be considered offensive to some readers. This book is for sale to adults ONLY.

Please store your files wisely where they cannot be accessed by underage readers.

* * * * * * * * * * * * * * * * * * *

WANT FREE COPIES OF MY BOOKS?
Just visit my blog and download free copies of my books:
http://angus-macgregor.awesomeauthors.org/angus-macgregor/

About the Publisher
4Fun Publishing, a member of **BLVNP Incorporated**, 340 S. Lemon #6200, Walnut CA 91789, info@blvnp.com / legal@blvnp.com
NOTE: Due to the highly emotional reaction of some people to works of erotic fiction, any email sent to the above address that contains foul language or religious references is automatically deleted by our anti-spam software and will not be seen. All other communications are welcome.

DISCLAIMER
Please don't be stupid and kill yourself. This book is a work of FICTION. Do not try any new sexual practice that you find in this book. It is fiction and not to be confused with reality. Neither the author nor the publisher or its associates assume any responsibility for any loss, injury, death or legal consequences resulting from acting on the contents in this book. Every character in this book is over 18 years of age. The author's opinions are not to be construed as the opinions of the publisher. The material in this book is for entertainment purposes ONLY. Enjoy.

In Close Quarters
Gay Mile-High Club Love Story

By: Angus MacGregor

© Angus MacGregor 2015
ISBN: 978-1-68030-584-5

Chapter 1

"Enjoy your flight, Mr. Jackson. Sorry we didn't have an upgrade for you," the ticket agent said in a weary but pleasant voice. "This red-eye is usually pretty open but not tonight. I got you a whole row at the very back of the plane though."

"That's fine, Susan. I appreciate it." Fred answered with a small grin. One perk of being a frequent flyer was getting to know most of the airline personnel. Nine times out of ten, he got upgraded or was given some perk. Tonight was one of those times it didn't look to work out. But a whole row was great. He could probably sleep a bit if he got in the right position. Though most of the time, he simply wasn't able to sleep unless he tossed back an Ambien before he boarded.

He made his way through the small airport terminal and waited for the one person in front of him going through the TSA checkpoint. Again, it was nice to see familiar faces. Almost all the time he was waved through without a look. He was pre-cleared on most flights and rarely took off his shoes anymore. He hadn't been through the small terminal in Tyler, Texas before and the hair on the back of his neck stood up as he moved through the line preparing for the inevitable questions. Fred slid his carry-on through the conveyor belt and stepped out of his loafers and put them in the bin along with his other personal items and walked through the scanner. It beeped as he knew it would.

"Excuse me, sir. Do you have something else in your pockets?" A thick-necked young man said. He looked all of twenty-one. He had a close cropped crew cut and bright blue eyes. His smile was enigmatic, part sincerely kind, part sinister.

"Hip replacement. Sets off the sensors sometimes." Fred said with a tired smile, patting his pockets to make sure all the rest of his personal items were removed.

"Can you go back through, sir and we will try it again," the young TSA agent said. Fred obeyed hearing the familiar chirp of the alarm as he walked back through a second time.

"Sir, will you come with me?"

"Why? I fly all the time. This is pretty routine for me. Can't you just use your wand or something?"

"Sir, just come with me. You have been randomly selected for a more thorough search for explosive residue as well as the concealed metal. It will just take a moment."

Fred felt his face flush with annoyance. He looked around. This hayseed airport was practically deserted. The only people around were the few sad souls looking to board this late night flight to DFW and on to PDX. Clearly, this guy was bored out of his mind or something. Normally, Fred would have asked for a supervisor or asserted his frequent-flyer status in some way. But he was just too tired tonight. He followed the muscular young man around the partition and through a hidden door. Once inside, the young man closed the door and flipped a lock.

"I'm going to need you to undress sir. Then I will do the explosive swab and search you for the unseen metal."

"Are you fucking kidding me?" Fred said stepping back from the young man. "I fly all the time. I have never been searched like this."

"It's just routine, sir. Once in a while, we randomly search frequent-flyers as well as others. Sorry for the inconvenience. It will just take a moment. You won't be late for your flight. Please go ahead and disrobe."

The young man was quiet, but totally authoritative. Fred swallowed and sat down his belongings, feeling his asshole clinch in worry. He looked around the small cubicle. There was no escape, no getting out of this. It was like a goddamn impromptu prostate exam or something.

"This is fucking ridiculous," he muttered, kicking off his shoes and reaching for the buttons to his wrinkled dress shirt. He hesitated for a moment, hoping this idiot would be telling him it was all a joke. But soon, Fred was unbuttoning his shirt and pulling it off. He added his white t-shirt to the pile. He unbuckled his belt and took a deep breath as he slid his dress slacks off and laid them on a table, standing in his Calvin Klein briefs and dark black socks. One look at the young man let Fred know he wasn't finished.

"Are you shitting me?" he said. Fred reached down and violently ripped off his socks and then defiantly pushed his underwear down to the floor and stepped out of them, handing them to the agent like a prize.

"Why don't you go ahead and take a big sniff of my shorts. Bet my sack is nice and sweaty for you," Fred hissed feeling the cool air-conditioned air swirl around his balls. His jaw was clenched as he tried to will his penis to behave and not react to the insane situation. The jock TSA agent seemed nonplussed by Fred's anger and simply moved around in front of him with a plastic wand with a square of soft fabric on the tip.

"I'm going to test you for explosive residue and then I will perform a search for the hidden metallic objects," he said robotically. His blue eyes looked deep into Fred's eyes. They twinkled with mirth. The agent took the wand and began to lightly draw it across Fred's palms and in between all of his fingers. The light, tingling sensation did not help deflect the inappropriate erection growing larger by the moment. As the agent finished with Fred's hands, he turned to a machine and placed the swab on the sensor. It registered negative. Fred exhaled and tried to imagine this intolerable inconvenience was over. The agent put on another swab and turned to face Fred. This time, he lightly traced the fabric up Fred's arm. He took Fred's hand and lifted his arm and ran the wand across the thick brown fur under his arms. Then the wand slid down his chest and across one nipple. Fred held his breath and stared. The agent continued to the other nipple, the soft fabric teasing and causing the pink nubbin to swell and stand at attention. He took Fred's other hand and lifted it, tracing his arm and armpit with the wand before moving to the machine to scan the fabric. Result: Negative.

The agent replaced the swab and turned to Fred. "What the fuck, dude? You think I took a bath in explosives before getting on a plane?"

The agent smirked but continued his methodical work, now sliding the wand across Fred's furry belly and down to his pubic bush. "You think I stuck my dick in some C4 or something, you asshole?" he barked. The agent's hand gripped Fred's hip as the wand lightly traced through the wreath of chestnut hair surrounding his penis before lightly running down the length of Fred's erection. The agent swirled the fabric against the thick drop of precum that hung from Fred's aroused cock before sliding around his heavy scrotum. He moved to the machine and deposited the swab into the sensor. Result: Negative. He placed another square on the wand.

"Please turn around, sir," the young man said with deep voiced authority. Fred shook his head and turned around, feeling the light tickle of the swab trace his shoulder blades, down his spine, and into his furry ass crack. The agent lightly touched his buttocks and pulled one cheek slightly apart before sliding the wand into the furry trench and across Fred's clenched hole. The tip touched his sack before pulling back.

"Christ," Fred snapped. Once again, the sensor read, negative. "Are we done?"

"With the explosives test, yes sir. Now I need to search you for hidden metallic objects. The agent moved behind Fred and began to touch his hair. "I am going to be touching you for a moment sir. I will try and be as quick and noninvasive as possible."

Fred could feel the man's warm hands slide across his thick dark brown hair and down the sides of his face and to his neck and shoulders. There was no cold latex feel of gloves, just his warm hands. He pulled Fred's arms up and reached around to feel his chest, sliding his hands across his nipples and down his hairy belly. Fred could feel the agent's shirt and trousers press against his naked flesh. An unmistakable bulge pressed into his ass as the agent continued his slow examination. The agent's hands slid down and lightly felt his pubic area before lightly gripping his penis and testicles in a firm grip. Fred gulped and closed his eyes.

"What are you doing, man?" he whispered.

"Just conducting a thorough search, sir," the agent spoke softly into his ear, his warm breath soft and wet on his face. The agent reached up and turned Fred around by his shoulders, his nose just a millimeter away. The agent stared hard into Fred's eyes as his hand continued to fondle Fred's leaking penis. His thumb ran across the tip. He brought the finger up to his lips and casually licked the honey. Fred gasped. The agent slid to his knees, his face an inch from Fred's cock. He lifted Fred's penis up against his belly and ran his fingers through his pubes and firmly gripped one testicle at a time before feeling underneath to Fred's taint, causing the man to spread his legs further apart. The agent quickly moved behind him. Fred's mind reeled. Why in the hell was he submitting to this? No one pushed him around. He was always in control, always the one calling the shots. And yet, here he was naked and docile, allowing a twenty-something year old jarhead to fondle his junk like a creepy coach.

"Go ahead and bend over, sir. We are almost done here," the deep voice ordered. Fred robotically obeyed, bending over the table, spreading his legs further apart. He shivered as a thick dollop of lube pressed against his asshole. A thick finger penetrated him, followed by a second, and then a third. The agent's face was literally pressing against his furry ass cheeks as the probing continued. Precum poured from his cock as the agent pushed again and again inside him. He was moments from orgasm.

Holy shit. Just go ahead and fuck me, Fred thought as the agent fingered him deeper and deeper, pressing against his prostate in an unrelenting rhythm. The agent's breathing was faster now. Suddenly, the fingers retreated. He heard the man's zipper open. The quiet of the room suddenly was filled with the smacking of skin on skin and a loud grunt, followed by hot liquid sliding down his ass crack and the weight of the agent press against him. Fred turned his head and saw the agent's thick penis, slick with semen, resting against his ass. The agent grabbed a handful of tissues and cleaned the tip of his large cock before sliding back into his pants and zipping. He gently wiped the wet residue from Fred's crack like a father cleaning his son's butt for a diaper change.

"Okay, Mr. Jackson. Looks like everything checks out. Sorry for the delay. You can get dressed now."

Fred turned around and stared at the man who looked flushed and somewhat smaller now that he had ejaculated. Fred was filled with confusion: rage and sexual frustration coursed through him, but one look into those blue eyes was totally disarming. He began to dress silently and as quickly as he could. As he finished sliding his feet back into his loafers, the agent moved closer again and gripped him by the arms.

"Really appreciate your cooperation, Mr. Jackson. That was my first time to conduct a thorough strip search like that. I hope you weren't too uncomfortable."

Fred shook his head. The agent pressed his hand against Fred's still hard cock and gripped it through his trousers. "You need me to take care of that before you leave?" he asked sincerely.

Most of Fred was screaming YES, goddammit! But instead he laid his land on the side of the young man's face and smiled. "No, I think I'll just hold on to this good feeling for a while. Fuck, buddy. That was intense to say the least."

The agent moved closer and lightly kissed Fred on the lips, warm and wet. "I'm Jason. Jason McCoy. If you need to get in touch with me or if I can help you out again. I would be glad to."

Fred tucked his shirt in again and smiled at the young man. "I will definitely remember you, Agent McCoy. Thanks for keeping me safe."

Chapter 2

Fred almost ran into the nearest men's room and locked himself in a stall. He hung his bag on the hook and slid his pants down and sat on the toilet, his hands visibly shaking. His dick was still hard and he wanted to cum. He pulled on his shaft and leaned back, envisioning Agent McCoy's hot load splashing on his ass. Fucking A, he thought. How the hell did that just happen? These feelings that had bubbled below the surface for so long in his life were roaring to life. That dude just released the Kraken in me, Fred thought sliding his hand back and forth on his penis watching the precum slick and wet on the round tip. He moved his hand over the honey and tasted the fluid. He milked out another drop and tasted it as well. Holy fuck he wanted to bust a nut. Someone came in the bathroom and it broke Fred's reverie. He just needed to get home and then figure this shit out.

Fred moved out of the bathroom and found a seat in the quiet terminal waiting for the short twenty-five minute commuter flight to DFW. He normally didn't take these late-night flights but he wanted to get home. He had already been on the road a week and he was sick of hotels and pretending to enjoy the banal conversations of business associates. He had been a traveling salesman for ten years now and he was tired. The money was pretty good and he actually did like the freedom of being his own boss most of the time.

There was no doubt that the constant traveling had most likely contributed to the end of his marriage. But there was more than just being gone all the time. He had gotten married right out of college. He had been completely in love with Sara and enjoyed being married and fucking her, even if he sometimes fantasized about a different kind of sex when they were humping. But the nights sitting naked on the couch together with his dick deep inside her pussy for an hour were distant memories. Three boys and fifteen years of marriage later, the magic had been replaced by ambivalence. But really, that wasn't true either. The truth was a real desire under the surface kept bubbling up and it simply was in directed conflict with being a married guy in a traditional marriage.

The feelings had been there even as a high school student. Hell, they were more than feelings. Fred had acted on them many times trying to find his way through his adolescence. He felt awake and alive when he indulged them, but the fact was, he had really loved all the sexual experiences of his youth before settling down with one sweet girl that he truly cared for with all his heart. But as the years went by, the ache and desires had bubbled up again and again. At first, he tried to push them down. Later, he rationalized that whatever he might be doing was allowed since it was just sex, and certainly nothing he could do with his wife. But soon, he noticed that the separations were almost happier than coming back home. The hostilities were bigger and he and Sara had simply become very good roommates, but no longer lovers.

It was somewhere along the line during one of his very long sales trips that Sara had found refuge from her loneliness and lack of intimacy with a neighbor. Chris was a good guy. He and his wife, Monica had gotten divorced two years earlier and he had stayed in the neighborhood. He was kind and funny, shit he was sexy as hell, Fred had to admit. The two of them had even had a moment in a tent a year earlier when they took their boys camping. It had been completely unexpected and was fucking amazing. Very funny looking back on it now. While he and Chris had been getting each other off, just a week before, Chris had been getting Sara off. It was one of the big ironies of life that both Fred and Sara were intimately acquainted with Chris's thick cock. They had even laughed about it, though at first, Fred found it a pretty hard revelation to handle. But he had figured, at least I know that the guy who is now fucking my ex-wife is really good at it.

That weekend with Chris had been experience number four in his adult life with another guy. He had slept with exactly one girl – Sara, in his whole life. They had fucked for the first time in college. Both of them had been twenty and they were good at fucking. He had never even been tempted to hook up with another woman. He was completely and utterly in love with Sara and loved being with her. No, that's not where all the temptations had been. Fred had pushed down all the desires that came to the surface with his friends and neighbors (like Chris) and the dozens and dozens of men who had hit on him while on the road in the past few years. It was pretty amazing how often it happened and was almost a miracle he hadn't acted on most of them. He didn't know if he was a pussy, still confused, or just lazy. And now he was forty, alone, divorced, and dreamed of finding a boyfriend. *Did it get more fucked up than that,* he thought.

"Good evening ladies and gentlemen. Flight 4580 service to DFW will begin boarding in five minutes."

Fred looked around and realized the boarding area was full of two dozen other tired travelers. He also noticed his dick was still profoundly hard and pressing against the thin fabric of his slacks. A skinny farm boy in faded Wranglers sat across from him, staring fixedly at his erection, slowly rubbing his crotch that was pressing hard against the tight denim. Fred adjusted his package which seemed to break the young man's concentration. His young face flushed red and he looked away. Fred spread his legs wider and watched the gaze move back to his crotch. Fred stood up and grabbed his bag. He smiled at the young man and stretched, enjoying the feeling of his cock pressing against his trousers even harder. What the fuck is up with me today, Fred thought.

"You think there's time to take a leak before this flight boards?" he asked the farm boy.

The boy stared and shrugged. "I guess so. Not a bad idea," he said in a low, quiet voice. Fred headed to the men's room feeling the young man following behind. He took a spot at the urinals and pulled out his dick to piss. The young man moved in beside him, interestingly right beside him. Farm boy fished his cock out of his tight pants and let it flop along with his balls in the cool air, a bright yellow stream splashing against the white porcelain. Fred put his hands on his hips and let his piss spray loudly into the urinal. He looked over at the farm boy who was casually sliding his fingers up and down on his thin cock. The boy boldly reached over and gripped Fred's cock and balls, jacking him back and forth.

"You wanna go in the stall?" farm boy offered.

"Yeah I do, but better not. Fuck man, you are sexy as shit," Fred said. "You pick old guys like me up all the time?"

Farm boy grinned continued fondling Fred's cock. "Yeah. Shit man, your dick is so big. Let me suck it."

Fred smiled and patted the young man on the side of the face. "You are killing me kid. Maybe another time."

"You can fuck me if you want," Farm Boy offered in a final plea.

"Jesus Christ, buddy. I sure wish I could. You have a great dick yourself and I bet you would be a hell of a good time. But nah, not in here. Be careful, okay. Don't want you to get busted." Fred slid his penis back into his shorts and zipped up. He leaned over and kissed the Farm Boy on the side of his head. "You are fucking hot, kid." He left the young man standing at the urinal as another traveler entered and pulled up beside the young man. Fred wondered if the kid was going to make a move on the next guy too.

Fred made his way to the last row of the plane. There were only two seats in the row, not enough to really stretch out and sleep, but then the flight was so damn short it didn't matter. He stowed his bag and settled into the seat, watching the other tired travelers fill the small plane. He rubbed his hands across the dark stubble on his cheeks and rubbed his tired eyes. Sure enough, Farm Boy was heading down the aisle, ducking his head to avoid hitting the lights in the ceiling. The young man's crotch was still packed full, his balls rolling from side to side as he walked decidedly toward Fred. But at the last moment, he pulled into the row just ahead of Fred beside a redneck fifty year old man in shorts and a t-shirt. Fred watched the man's gaze find the Farm Boy's full crotch as he neared. The young man pushed passed the man to sit on the window seat, his tight denim ass rubbing the man in the face as he stepped over. The older man didn't seem to mind. The flight attendant closed the doors. Fred felt annoyed as he saw this plane was not nearly as full as the ticket agent had led him to believe.

The plane took off and the interior lights were dimmed. Fred could just make out the older man and the farm boy in the row diagonally from him. There was no one in the row ahead of Fred or in the two rows ahead of Farm boy. The flight attendant was back in the jump seat reading a book. So much for any service on this flight, he thought. Fred leaned his head back and closed his eyes. So tired, he thought. A turbulence bump shook Fred awake and he looked around. He saw the fifty year old traveler in front of him with his legs stretch wide into the aisle. The top of a baseball cap bobbed up and down above the man's lap, peeking out from the blanket discretely in his lap. Fred smiled. That fucking kid got some dick after all, he thought. Fred watched the older man's hand pressing on Farm Boy's head and then his neck stretched and his feet tensed, obviously sending a thick load of nut into Farm Boy's mouth. The kid had skills for sure. It was fast and discreet and the next thing Fred knew, the tall young man was sitting beside the older man again. He looked back at Fred with a sly grin and opened his mouth, sticking out his tongue. Fred smiled and gave the kid a thumbs up. *Shit, I think I missed a great opportunity there,* he thought. The fifty-year old man disappeared under the blanket and into Farm Boy's lap. Fred watched the young man's head lean back as he got sucked off. His mouth opened into a comic O-face as he shot his farm boy spunk into the man's hungry mouth. The man sat back up, wiping his mouth with the back of his hand. He turned around and Fred smiled knowingly. The man's eyes were wide in surprise, but he shrugged and smiled and turned back around and shifted close to Farm Boy so they were touching for the rest of the flight.

Chapter 3

Fred's cock was leaking into his shorts now and he figured he was going to have a big wet spot by the time he got to DFW. Fuck, he needed some goddamn dick. He was tired of always being so afraid and careful. This was what happened all the time: he was offered some amazing opportunity but he chickened out and didn't seize the day. Even the few times he had experienced gay sex, he practically talked himself out of it before it happened.

He made his way through the terminal to his departure gate. It looked like this flight was going to be more packed than normal too even at midnight. Fuck, he thought. Just what I need. He approached the ticket counter with apprehension. He saw Maureen working the desk and smiled.

"Tell me you can help me out here today, sweetheart," Fred said in his most ingratiating tone.

"Hi Fred. This flight is a fucking mess," she said under her breath. I don't have any first class upgrade for you, I'm afraid. In fact, it's stupidly full tonight. But if I put you on the back row, the three rows in front of you are all empty because the seats are all fucked up and they are being replaced so we have blocked them off. You would be back there pretty much all alone."

"Pretty much?" Fred said skeptically.

"Most of the other seats are full and I have one standby I need to throw on so he will be back there too, but one's not too bad I hope."

"He's not some weirdo or smelly meth-head is he? "

Maureen laughed. "That's always the way, isn't it? No, I think this guy will be pretty normal. He's a soldier."

"Really? Okay, well far be it from me to be a dick to America's best. Thanks for taking care of me, dear. And you never know, he hasn't checked in so he might not show."

"Always, Freddie. They aren't doing any service on this flight either so grab a water or something before you get on. I swear it's getting as bad as Spirit on our flights these days."

Fred smiled and patted Maureen's hand. He found an open store and grabbed a water and a Snickers bar. His stomach rumbled but he didn't dare try and eat something bigger this late. He just wanted to get home. He wanted a hot shower and to lay on his bed with the iPad and jerk off to Tumblr. Then sleep for a week. He found a bathroom and took another piss, no Farm Boy fun this time either. He inwardly kicked himself for being so damn timid. How many chances like that does the universe give you?

The boarding call was made and Fred made his way down the narrow center aisle toward the very back of the plane. Normally he absolutely hated the tail seats, but he wanted some space for some shuteye and a general buffer zone away from everyone. He smiled as he made his way down the aisle seeing the yellow caution tape across the back rows of seats that had maintenance issues. He stowed his bag and collapsed into the seat. He liked that the galley and lavatories in this plane were further up. He really was the only guy back here and that would be great. He pulled out his noise-canceling Beats by Dre and got ready to snooze away with his hand in his pants all the way home.

"Are you going to be okay back here all alone?" a smooth voice said above him. Fred looked up.

"Oh hey, Henry. Yeah I think this is just what the doctor ordered," Fred answered the short, solid flight attendant. The man's red-brown hair was perfectly styled as usual along with his uniform being in perfect order. His lightly freckled hand rested on Fred's shoulder. "Can you fuck up the seats on all my flights so I can have a private hidey-hole back here?"

"I'll see what I can do," Henry said with a smirk.

"Shit, I can take my pants off back here and no one will know," Fred added flirting with the man. He had enjoyed Henry's stares to his ass or junk more than once and had masturbated thinking of the flight attendant's certain to be red bush in his face.

Henry leaned close enough for Fred to smell his very light cologne. "Baby, if you slide your pants off, I will be back here to help you out in no time," Henry said with a wicked grin. "I've wanted to see your bad boys for a long time, now."

Fred flushed but smiled broadly. "Why they hell don't we get together on one of these layovers then."

"Oh, you know…" Henry waggled a silver wedding band in his face. "But you know, Steven and I have some pretty lax rules about all that. Maybe it's time for us to get real acquainted?"

Fred grinned and brazenly adjusted his still chubbed up cock which drew Henry's attention. "Oh my God," he whispered. "You are so bad, Fred. I'm gonna have to text Steven and see if I can get a pass. I need to see that bad boy in person." Henry looked around. "Gotta go. Now look at what you've done," he said pushing down on his own growing bulge that clearly showed off a round circumcised head through his khaki colored trousers. Fred smiled and grabbed his basket again.

"Mmm, that's what I'm talking about," he said in a whisper. He stared hard at Henry's round ass as he walked quickly up the aisle. He was not used to overt flirting like that and he had to admit, he really liked that. *What do you know, I wasn't too damn shy to play for once*, he thought. Fred put his headphones on and let his ears fill to the sounds of Ed Sheeran's "Sing."

Chapter 4

He was so tired. It didn't take long for his mind to fill with images of Henry's smooth, lightly ginger ass cheeks to appear in front of him so he could lightly trace the golden hairs in the warm crack with his tongue down to his pink pucker, sucking on his ass until he was moaning and spreading his legs wide to give Fred more access to his hole. In his mind, he reached underneath Henry's legs and pulled his hard cock back toward his mouth and swallowed the swollen tip all the way to his soft red pubes. A shadow passed in front of his closed eyes and he opened to find a dark form blocking the dim glow from the cabin lights. A frown crossed Fred's face and he slid the headphones from his ears.

"Damn, you look pretty comfortable back here. Sorry to mess up your special seat. I bet you were looking forward to stretching out and sleeping. I think the whole plane is full except for one of your seats here."

Fred's mouth fell open as he took in the passenger speaking to him. The man was solid and huge, at least 6'4". Close-cropped sandy blond hair covered his large head. His eyes were large, aquamarine, with long lashes that belonged on a supermodel. His jaw was square, like his shoulders that filled up the small space in the airplane like The Hulk. It was like looking at J.J. Watt in desert fatigues. Henry's small head peered around the colossus in front of Fred.

"Sorry Freddy. We are completely full. Need to squeeze this soldier back here with you. Hope you don't mind," Henry said with a glee in his eye that didn't hide his wicked sense of humor.

Fred pulled his legs over so that the soldier could slide into the seat beside him. The guy was so big, he had to wiggle his legs into the tight confines of the seat. "Man, they just don't make these things for a guy like me."

"There aren't that many guys like you," Fred said awestruck. He stuck his hand out. "Fred. Welcome to the back of the bus."

"Adam," the soldier replied with a massive hand that squeezed just hard enough. "Too bad we can't throw those broken seats out. We could lay down on the damn floor back here."

Fred swallowed and felt his dick twitch. "Yeah. That would make this flight a whole lot better." The soldier's leg rested closely against his own. The young man tried to move it away, but it was hopeless. "Pretty sure there is no way for us to not be all touchy feely back here. No worries, it doesn't bug me."

"Thank goodness, man. 'Cause I don't see any way we won't be rubbing against each other the whole damn flight. Like being back in a fuckin' foxhole."

"Bet that's true. Oh well, band of brothers and all that, right. You're probably used to close quarters."

"You can say that. Hard to even find time to rub one off with your buddy two inches away from you."

"Unless he gives you a hand," Fred said instantly regretting it.

Adam leaned close. "They still kind of frown on all that, so much for social evolution, right?" he said with a big grin.

His heavy, muscled arm rested tightly against Fred. Fred swallowed again and tried to will his cock to behave. It was hopeless. Fred tried to nonchalantly push it back down, but the damn thin trousers he was wearing were no help at all. *I might as well be fucking naked*, he thought looking at the mushroom outline of his cut dick press against the fabric. The plane was pushed back and began to taxi toward the runway. The cabin lights were turned off and the two men sat in the darkness. Adam leaned over.

"My johnson does exactly the same thing, always at the worst time. No worries, brother. You got a big dick," he whispered with that big grin again. Fred's face was scarlet.

"I need some loose pants like yours, buddy," Fred said.

"Yeah. I can be at full salute and you can hardly tell in these mo-fos. But trust me, it's about the same," he said gripping the sand-colored camouflage pants at the crotch and lightly waggling his junk. *Impressive was not nearly descriptive enough*, Fred thought looking at the manly lump Adam fisted in his big hands. "Sorry man, I get a little antsy on these flights. Didn't mean to offend."

"You didn't, Adam. I kind of enjoyed that," Fred said with a laugh. He reached down and patted the young man's knee. Adam looked at him and shoved his shoulder into Fred's a bit harder.

"Cool. Wish my CO was that understanding. He gives me shit all the time about being too touchy."

"Maybe he's a big closet case," Fred said.

"You have no idea."

The plane accelerated off the runway and moved into its cruising altitude. Fred looked at the lights below grow small and finally become only tiny pinpoints on the dark canvas of the night as they sped out of Texas toward the Rockies. Fred could smell the soap and a tiny bit of sweat from the soldier beside him. The young man's thigh was pressed hard against his. The air from the air conditioning was blasting arctic air on both of them. It felt good for a while then began to be a bit too much. Adam reached up to turn the controller down, but it didn't stop the flow of cold air in the least.

"This fucker is broken," he muttered. "It's colder than a witch's tit in here…and I'm never cold."

"Look, there is actual white frost on the damn thing," Fred said. He looked around and found a blanket still in the plastic wrap. "You want to share the blanket, big guy?"

Adam frowned for a moment and then chuckled. "Might as well. We're sitting close enough to give each other a handy anyway. Sorry man, I keep saying stupid shit like that."

"No worries, soldier. Kinda nice to not be all PC all the time, right?"

"You can say that again. Okay, crack that fucker open and get me warm, mister," Adam said with a laugh. Fred opened the blanket and spread it wide over the two of them, settling in again against the big man's shoulder. Fred searched for something new to say as the quiet became more uncomfortable.

"So you been in Afghanistan?"

"Yep, Kabul for a year. Thank God that's done. I am so ready to move on. I like the military but I miss home, you know. And to be honest, I've just been lonely and ready to come back and get on with life. Being deployed is kind of like being in a really good jail sometimes. I can't even remember the last time I had a day to myself. Even when I would get leave and shit, it was always with another few guys. And you know, I love them. They are my brothers in every way. But sometimes, you just want to be able to jack off without having to give your neighbor a tug at the same time."

Fred laughed. "I bet. It was like that with my kids and all when they were younger. Just couldn't get a free moment to look at some porn or rub one off or anything."

"You got kids? How many? Boys, girls?"

"Three boys – oldest is fifteen and thirteen year old twins."

"Oh shit. That is a lot of testicles around the house."

"You got that right. I think that's one reason me and the wife split up. She just needed a break from all the dongs." Fred said with a laugh.

"So, they live with you?"

"We still share them, but they mostly just stay with her and her new man when I am on the road. The rest of the time I have them. They don't get along with mom very well these days."

"So what happened? I mean, sounds like you were married a nice long time." Adam asked.

Fred shrugged. "Life, you know. We were crazy in love for a long time, but I was gone a lot. I think she got tired of waiting for me to settle down. We pretty much stopped having sex, having the kids and a busy life and all that. She found someone else with me being away all the time. Someone who made her happy I think."

"You know this guy that she hooked up with?"

"Yeah. He was our neighbor. We were friends too. Pretty close actually. Guess she and he got closer though."

Adam gave Fred a long, calculated look. Under the blanket, the young man moved his hand toward Fred's and touched it. "You figured out you like guys more than girls?"

"How did you pick up on that?" Fred asked incredulously.

"You know, that ole gaydar thing we have sometimes. Shit, most guys would not be cool with a big ox like me rubbing right against them without even trying to move away. I take it she knows?"

Fred smiled. "Yeah, I mean she tells me she always knew. But we still had good sex. I mean, we fucked all the time. Guess I was pretty good at it since we had the boys and everything. But we would go long times sometimes with nothing and I suppose she got tired of waiting."

"Were you playing with some sausage on the side?"

Fred nodded. "A little. Most of that happened when I was out on the road. Pretty easy to get picked up in a hotel bar these days, even for a guy like me."

"I wouldn't think a guy like you would have any trouble at all."

"Oh really? That's pretty high praise coming from Mr. Perfect."

Now it was Adam's time to laugh. "You know what they say – looks can be deceiving. I've got my own shit load of baggage just like everyone else."

"That's pretty hard to believe, but okay. So are you like out to all the other soldier guys in your unit?"

"You know, not really. I think quite a few of them wonder and maybe suspect. But I don't try and hook up with any of them. I mean, it has happened a few times but mostly it was all drunken goofing around that got out of hand a few times. Most of the guys I fucked around with probably either wouldn't remember or at least wouldn't admit it. I've had like three actual gay dates where I knew the guys were interested and all that. One of those turned into a three month relationship. Not very long. I just don't like people nosing into my shit. I'm not ashamed or anything, it's just complicated and easier in the military to pretend. But I'm really tired of it."

Fred reached over and took Adam's large, warm hand in his under the blanket and lightly squeezed it. The soldier pushed his shoulder softly into Fred's and squeezed back. Fred lightly traced the man's thick, strong fingers with his thumb.

"No judging from me, buddy. Look at me, forty years old and still in the closet for the most part. I'm like you, just haven't been able to wave the rainbow flag yet. Not ashamed either, but I don't like the questions or comments. Guess we are just a couple of lost boys or something. So, did you ever like girls at all?"

"Yeah. I mean I dated girls in high school. Girls loved me. I got a bunch of hand jobs and blow jobs, most of them really bad. I got pretty good getting girls off with my hands, but eating pussy just made me gag. I know most guys are so into it, but I would get all freaked out with all that pink, frilly shit down there, not to mention weird smells and all. But for the most part, the girls were no good taking care of me either. And once I was brave enough to do it with a guy, I just knew. Even when I was a kid, I always fantasized about fucking boys instead of girls usually."

"That sounds just like me. I never had sex with any girl other than my wife. I liked it but when I fantasized or looked at porn or spanked it, I was always thinking of a guy."

"How old were you the first time you tried it?"

"I was thirteen, with a sixteen year old neighbor. "

"Damn, just like me. I was twelve with a sixteen year old Eagle Scout in a tent."

"Sweet. Mine was sharing a sofa bed in the family room while we were watching movies. Wrestling turned into tickling and then into groping. I didn't know what the hell was going on, but I sure loved it."

"Nice. I woke up to find my Eagle Scout buddy groping me while he was jerking off. It didn't freak me out or anything. I think my balls dropped when I was in fifth grade or something. The next night he tried to fuck me, but I was bigger than him and ended up the top guy, even though I really didn't know what the hell to do. Nature just sorted that out," Adam said with a smile, rubbing his middle finger in and out of a circle of his thumb and forefinger.

"Shit. Boys sure can get with it if they are curious, huh? Too bad I wasn't your scouting buddy. We might never have left that tent," Fred said. His hand was damp now, his fingers lightly entwined with the soldiers.

"Well you boys look pretty cozy back here," Henry said moving down the aisle with the drink cart. "Can I get you guys something to drink before we all turn in for the rest of the flight?" His smirk was devilish as he sized up the men sharing the blanket.

"Well you have practically frozen us," Fred snapped. "If I didn't have America's Best back here warming me up my dick would fall off."

"Oh honey, I am sure he could help with that too," Henry offered complete with a Z-snap. "You need some water or something?"

"I'll take some water," Adam said. "Don't you want some?" he asked Fred.

"Yeah, probably a good idea."

Henry handed them small cups of water and smiled. "Okay fellows. Unless you need me to tuck you in, I'll leave you alone for the rest of the flight."

"Thanks, Henry," Fred said smiling. "We can tuck one another in."

I bet you will too," Henry said looking back over his shoulder as he pushed the cart back to the galley and stowed it.

"That guy seems pretty gay," Adam whispered.

"Oh yeah. He's been hitting on me for a long time."

"You ever...?"

"No, but he certainly offered. It's just normally when we are headed to PDX, I am ready to get in the car and get home."

"I bet he's pretty crazy in the sack. Little guys like him can be pretty wild."

"Might be. He always has a boner that's for sure."

"Don't' we all," Adam said moving Fred's hand to his crotch, pressing it against his erection.

"Shit, soldier. At ease." Fred said allowing himself a quick feel before moving his hand back. Adam's hand moved over to his lap and softly squeezed his bulge, rubbing his cock through the thin fabric of his trousers. Fred spread his legs wider to allow the soldier more access. He closed his eyes and exhaled.

"Damn, Dad. You got some major meat there," Adam whispered.

"Oh buddy. Don't start something you aren't gonna finish. I might look tough but I'm a pussy when it comes to guys fucking around with me just for fun."

Adam moved his hand to Fred's thigh and rubbed it back and forth. "You don't have to worry, Dad. I'm not trying to mess you around. Just a flirty fuck, especially with a hot guy like you. When all the other gay boys were trying to find the youngest, tightest piece of ass they could, I was back in my bunk jerking off thinking of boning my CO. Just got a thing for an older man, I guess."

"That's the first time I have ever been glad someone told me I was an older man," Fred said letting his hand rest on Adam's muscled thigh. *The heat coming off this soldier is like uranium*, he thought. I feel like I have known you a long time for some reason."

"Like one of the boys that used to come mow your yard."

"You could have been one of those boys for sure. Holy shit."

"I used to drive my neighbor crazy I think. Mowing his yard without my shirt on. I would sit in his garage on this old couch afterwards, my shorts all low and showing my ass crack. I would wear these cut off sweats with no underwear. I would sit there with my legs all spread wide, rubbing my sack while he watched. The guy would stare and get so hard. He had a bathroom in the garage with a shower. A few times, he offered it to me to clean up, like I didn't have a shower next door in my own house. But a few times, I just went ahead and showered right there in front of him. He would stand there and talk to me while I cleaned up. I would soap up my dick and balls for five minutes while he watched. He didn't even try to act like he was looking somewhere else. He would just stare and watch me wash up, rubbing his dick the whole time. I was a monster, just loving driving him crazy."

"I have a feeling if he was anything like me, seeing you all soapy and beautiful like that, would have filled up the spank bank for years. I think it's kind of sweet you gave him such a huge memory. It's not like he got in the shower with you, though I bet he thought hard about it."

"I even invited him in. I was terrible. That poor guy. I was like jail bait of the worst kind. Really glad he had some self-control. I would go home and jerk off imagining him in the shower with me. I was desperate for an older guy to touch me. I was like walking kryptonite for any weak-willed, sexually curious man. I'm probably very lucky I didn't end up in a real mess. Or worse, mess up some poor man's life just because I was a huge horn dog."

"Well that still wouldn't have been your fault as a young man. But yeah, probably great it just remained a fantasy. Sounds like fun role-play material now though," Fred added giving the soldiers thick thigh a squeeze. "So other than the Eagle Scout, did you play with other boys growing up?"

"Oh fuck yeah. I made it with half the guys on my high school football and baseball team. Well, not really, but a fair amount. I kind of just had this charm I think. If the guy was the least bit curious or horned up, I was usually able to get into his pants. I fucked like fifteen guys from my school."

"You actually fucked them?" Fred asked.

"Most of them. At least half of them boned me too. Plenty of blow jobs and hand jobs along the way too. But I was pretty skilled and sliding into home plate with my dick. Even guys that didn't roll like that at all ended up with me balls deep in them. Sometimes just once, a few of the guys I fucked a dozen times."

"Shit. I would have loved that. I did fool around like three times in high school. Swapping head and tried fucking. It was great. I knew I loved it back then but just sort of chalked it up to teenage curiosity and horniness. But even after I got married, I kept reimagining all the dicks. I just knew that was what I really wanted the most. I just never met anyone who was right, you know. I mean, I've had some fun here and there. But mostly, I've been lonely for so long." Fred sighed and looked out the window at the deep darkness and the blink of the lights on the aircraft wing. "It's weird, even when you are surrounded by people, you can still be so fucking lonely. It's the opposite of what it's been like for you I guess. You are ready to have some alone time."

Adam looked into Fred's eyes, long and deep, seemingly trying to read his whole life history in the gaze. He slid his large, warm hand around Fred's. The men stared at one another for a minute or two, not speaking, just soaking in the connection. Finally Adam spoke.

"I'm not looking to be alone. I just need less noise, less chaos and fucking danger."

Fred smiled and traced the soldier's fingers with his thumb as he sat so close he could feel the heat radiating off the young man's body against his. "I don't think you are going to have any problem finding a long line of boys ready to spend time with you. I have a feeling you will have your pick."

Adam shrugged. "What if I'm not looking for a boy? I've been sleeping and eating and pissing with boys for years now. Don't get me wrong...I love seeing them naked. I love how they are strong and hard and always horned up. But at the end of the day, they really don't interest me. Too much drama and they are so fucking immature. I like spending time with a dad much more. I wish my own dad wanted to spend time to me, but not in bed..." both men laughed. "But just to hang with him, get to know him more. I was a total shit to him when I was growing up, mostly because I just thought he didn't get me and obviously didn't approve of me, even though I wasn't out or anything. He knew, you know?"

"Why are you so sure?" Fred asked. He cautiously moved his finger free of Adam's hand and moved it back over to the young man's lap, rubbing his penis that was still thick and hard against his fatigues. Adam spread his long legs wider apart and laid his head back against the headrest. Fred gripped the large shaft and then moved to the full sack below and let his fingers rub against the golf ball sized testicles.

"He walked in on me a couple of times. Right when I was balls deep in a teammate or joined up in a 69. Once he even walked in with me on my belly, a big offensive lineman blowing his nut in my hole. I remember his face. He stood there watching then looked at me with disgust and left. He never talked about it, but I knew he was embarrassed and judged me big time. He always acted like everything was fine but it was right beneath the surface like some killer undertow. Even when I signed up and headed to Afghanistan, he didn't say much. Part of me thought he didn't care if I came back or not."

"I know that's probably not the case. I have a feeling he loves you like crazy. Some dads just can't figure out the whole gay thing. If I was a betting man, I bet he might even think some of your feelings came from him and he's embarrassed about that."

"You think my dad likes dick? I really doubt that."

"I wouldn't know but it's not impossible, even if he keeps a tight lid on it. I'm pretty sure my own dad had some experiences with a fishing buddy of his. I don't have any direct evidence to that. It's more of a sense now that I've had some experiences of my own and thinking back to all those trips he took, staying in a small tent together, some comments from his friend about skinny dipping, you know, things like that. At least to me, I like the idea that he fooled around some himself."

"Have you just asked him?"

"Can't. He's gone now. Wish I had though." Fred said. He continued to stroke Adam's shaft under the blanket. His own shorts were wet with precum now and Adam's big hand moved over to his crotch again. Fred reached in and slid his zipper down. A moment later, Adam had his cock pulled out and was rubbing his thumb over the oozing tip.

"Damn, Dad. You've got some juice leaking out there for sure." The soldier said pulling his hand back and sliding his finger into his mouth, tasting the honey.

Adam reached down and unfastened his own pants and pulled his erection out. Fred's hand gripped the soft, swollen shaft, sliding his hand up and down slowly as the two men leaned into one another's shoulders and fondled each other. Fred leaned his head to the side and Adam's head lightly touched his. Their breathing increased as they stroked one another. Fred rolled the young man's large testicles in his fingers, smooth and silky in the loose sack. All he could think of was putting those balls in his mouth. Adam read his mind.

"Bet you want to suck those balls, Dad. Fuck," he whispered," I want to feed you my cock so bad."

"It's all I want, son," Fred replied. *When did this turn into a dad-son role-play thing?*

A teenage looking boy was moving up the aisle toward the lav located six rows in front of the men. As he neared, he stared at the men and broke into a big smile, complete with a thumbs up as he pushed the door open and went inside. The look unnerved Fred.

"We better cool it. Did you see that kid? He knew we were fucking around back here."

"Nah. Even if he did, he's just jealous he can't join in."

Fred pulled his hand away and pushed his hard dick back inside his slacks and settled back, a bit further from Adam in his seat. Adam let the blanket drop, his large erection laying against his tan t-shirt, a large wet stain blooming around it. He flipped his penis back and forth, dangerously out in the open before pushing it back inside his pants.

"Blue balls for both of us I guess," he chuckled.

"True words, soldier," Fred said. "You want to try and get a little sleep?"

"Yeah, I can sleep anywhere. You okay if I lean on you? I probably will if I fall asleep."

"Don't mind at all, buddy."

Chapter 5

Fred pulled his headphones up on his head and let them pair up again and listened to Sam Hunt singing "Take Your Time." Fatigue took over and he fell into a deep sleep almost immediately. His mind drifted back in time. He was on the road again sitting in another dim hotel bar nursing an Old Fashioned made with Pendleton whiskey, one of his favorite drinks. He was tired and needed sleep, but he was feeling something else too. He was tired of jerking off alone. He wanted someone else to touch him, to want to be with him. Even when he and Sara fucked, which was damn rare these days, she seemed distant and he was acting himself. It wasn't hateful or mean, it just wasn't very inspired. It was nice to come, but it was a far cry from when they had first married.

He knew he bore the greatest share of this failure. Little by little he was coming to terms with the fact he simply was more attracted to men these days. He had no problem getting hard when he looked at gay porn or masturbated thinking of a co-worker. Sex with Sara was hit and miss these days. He smiled wistfully thinking of sleepovers and barn campouts with other horny boys that ended up with his hand around another boy's dick or sliding inside a friend's mouth as he did the same. Those boyhood experimentations had started to come to his mind more and more these days. Shit, he wondered if any of those guys ever thought about it like he did.

"You look like how I feel, buddy," a voice beside him said.

Fred turned and saw another businessman: white shirt, loosened tie, rumpled and tired. The man was smaller than he was. Solid and dark, thick black curly hair and a day's growth of beard. His dark blue eyes sparkled in the dim light as did his white teeth as he grinned and raised his glass toward Fred.

"Bill Rentuccio," he said. "Can I buy you another?"

Fred smiled and offered his hand. "Sure, man. I could drink another. Thanks. I'm Fred."

"You bet. Bartender, two more here," he said throwing $20 on the bar. "You here for the convention too?"

"Yeah, this place is pretty full of us, even if we were too cheap to stay at the venue hotel."

"Fuck that $300 a night for a shitty room. We've got that here for $150," Bill said taking a big gulp of his beer.

"You can say that again."

"And it all pretty much looks the same when the lights are out and you are lying in the bed rubbing one off to HGTV before bed."

Fred almost spit out his drink. "You spank it watching 'Property Virgins?'"

"Hell no. I hate that bitch. Gotta be Chip from 'Fixer Upper' or 'Property Brothers.'"

Fred laughed. "Yeah, that Chip is quite the charmer. And Joanna is really hot."

"Yeah, I mostly just pay attention to him."

Fred's radar was barely working but he was picking up some signals. Just for the hell of it, he spread his legs a bit wider on the barstool until his right leg barely touched Bill's. The man did not move his leg. He held it still and continued drinking.

"He's just got that southern charm, you know. And that ex-jock football player thing that I think is pretty cool."

"And he looks pretty good in those Carhartt's too," Fred added.

"Exactly," Bill said turning to him. "See, you get it too. A real man's man." Bill's leg pressed just a small bit harder against Fred's. "Kind of the same when I am watching football. You see some amazing athlete like Tom Brady or Brett Favre and you just sort of want to take them right into your mouth, you know?"

Fred froze with a stunned expression on his face. "Uh yeah. Right down to the short-curlies."

Bill laughed. "Abso-fuckin-lutely. I'm not ashamed to say I would gobble down his bone and drink the gravy if he was my friend."

Fred shook his head and smiled. "Well I haven't thought of it exactly like that, but I wouldn't kick him out of bed either."

"That's what I say. See, my wife thinks I'm so in love with all these athletes, but I just respect the hell out of them and besides, I think they are fucking amazing. I bet they are way more exciting in bed than most bitches and a lot less needy."

"Maybe so," Fred said.

"So who would you let fuck you, if it meant you would be their friend and get to hang with them and everything? Some famous guy, who would you bend over for?"

"Uh, I don't know. I think I have never thought of that. Not sure. What about you?"

"Well, I'd let Elvis fuck me for one. Maybe Bill Clinton. And Wally, from Leave it to Beaver."

Fred snorted. "Holy shit, dude. That is messed up. But yeah, those are pretty sexy guys. I think I would pick Harrison Ford or the guy who played Aragorn on Lord of the Rings."

"Viggo Mortenson."

"Yeah, him. Oh and all the guys from Friday Night Lights...especially Coach Taylor," Fred added getting into the spirit of the conversation.

Bill tapped the neck of his beer bottle on Fred's glass. "Clear eyes..."

"Full Hearts."

"Can't lose. Oh hell yeah. Coach Taylor could bend me over any time he wanted," Bill said. "Bet he loved watching Tim Riggins in the showers," Bill said in a way too loud voice.

"Dude, you are crazy," Fred said in a low whisper looking around to see if anyone was listening to this insane conversation. No one was. "So, Bill. You're talking a lot about banging guys. You ever do that in real life?" Fred held his breath for the inevitable shutdown or explosion.

"Sure. Life's too short to not try shit out, don't you think? I mean, there aren't a million gays out there fucking each other because it feels bad."

"Guess you're right there."

"What about you, buddy? You ever smoked a bone or rubbed one off with a friend?" This time Bill's voice was somewhat subdued.

"Ah you know, back in school. Kid stuff, experimenting. Was pretty fun actually."

"Oh hell yeah. I had a next door neighbor that definitely showed me the ropes when I was in high school. I enjoyed that as much as my first pussy. Maybe more."

Fred nodded. "I had some of those too."

"You ever get the urge to rub your dick against another one since then?"

Fred smiled and took a long drink.

"Well, that's a yes. Come on."

"Excuse me?"

Bill threw a $10 on the bar and jumped down from the barstool. "Let's go, buddy. Let's make a new memory," Bill said quietly as he slid his hand dangerously up Fred's thigh with a squeeze at the end.

"Ah, that's okay man. I was just kidding around," Fred said looking around.

Bill stood looking at him with a smirk, continuing to rub his hand on Fred's thigh, oblivious to anyone paying attention. They still weren't.

"Well, I hope you change your mind," Bill said tossing a business card onto the bar. He took a pen from his pocket and wrote 504 on the back of the card. He patted Fred on the back and left.

Fred drained his drink and picked up the card and studied it. Seemed like Bill Rentuccio was an interesting guy to say the least. *Damn*, Fred thought, *he sure didn't hold back.* Fred reached down and adjusted his junk which was hard and leaking. *Jesus, I am so fucked up.* He picked up his suit coat and threw it over his shoulder and headed to the elevator. He pushed the 8th floor button and leaned against the wall, absentmindedly pushing down his erection while his mind raced. He looked up when the car stopped allowing a guest to get off. As he looked up, he saw he was on the 5th floor. In a split second he pushed through the closing doors into the corridor. He walked down the carpeted hallway and stopped in front of 504. Before he could knock, the door opened. Bill was standing in front of him with his white shirt and briefs and black socks.

"Glad you changed your mind," he said. He let Fred into the room. The only light was the glow of the television and the sparkle of lights from the Las Vegas strip. "Take off your pants and stay a while," he said handing Fred a beer from the mini fridge. Fred grinned and took the drink, noticing the prominent bulge in Bill's briefs, along with his dark hairy legs making him look like 'Risky Business' Tom Cruise.

Fred sat on the bed and kicked off his shoes thinking this felt completely normal and completely alien all at the same time. Bill moved close to Fred in between his legs. He was practically at the same level as Fred's head now that he was seated. The man moved even closer, close enough that Fred could smell the Polo cologne mixed with sweat and a whiff of smoke. His dark eyebrows were thick and black, framing his blue eyes. His nose was only an inch away and his warm breath blew softly over his face. Bill's scratchy cheek rubbed against Fred's and his lips hovered close. Fred reached up and gripped Bill's neck and pulled him in and pressed his lips tightly against the man's. They were warm and thick. They opened and Fred's tongue probed inside just enough to find Bill's tongue. They kissed long and hard, rubbing and groping one another until Bill pushed Fred back and on the bed and climbed on top of him. Fred pulled the man tightly to him feeling Bill's erection dig into his belly and rub against his own hardness. Bill kissed him deeply, his scratchy face making Fred grow even more aroused as their faces rubbed against one another. Bill tore at Fred's clothes, pulling at his shirt and pants until Fred broke away from the kisses and pulled his buttoned shirt over his head and pushed his slacks down. Bill gripped his penis through his underwear and kneaded it with his small, strong hands as the men continued to grind and rub against one another.

Bill pulled away and gripped the elastic on Fred's boxer briefs and pulled them quickly down. It caused his hard cock to smack against his lightly furry belly with a soft thwack. The smaller man was on his knees beside Fred's head, his fat cock bulging in the pouch of his briefs. In a sexy wiggle, Bill slid them down off his furry ass. He moved quickly and straddled Fred's face with his hairy thighs, his full sack rubbing against Fred's face. Bill stretched out on Fred's belly and swallowed his penis in one motion all the way to his brown pubes. Fred's eyes rolled back. He looked up and began to probe and lick Bill's sack and swallowed one ball then the other, bathing them with his tongue. Then Bill pulled back and his fat, five inch cock penetrated his lips and slid deep into this throat as the men sucked and swallowed and fellated one another with abandon.

***

A sudden jolt of turbulence jarred Fred awake from his excellent dream. But his momentary annoyance from being evicted from the sensual memory was quickly replaced by the growing realization that he was moments away from a full orgasm, the kind that soaks your belly and shorts with a thick load of cream. He peered down at his lap and saw the bobbing form under the blanket and realized a hot, wet mouth was sucking his cock like a pro. The blond crew cut appeared from beneath the blanket, wiping his mouth with the back of his hand.

"You need to follow me. I'm going into the bathroom. Wait ten seconds and follow me. Don't think about this, Dad. Just do it," Adam said with authority.

Chapter 6

Fred watched the big backside of the soldier move silently up to the lavatory and disappear within. His heart was beating like a drum in his chest. Fred looked around. The plane was quiet and still. He pushed his penis back inside his slacks and eased out of his seat and moved into the aisle and nervously pushed the bi-fold door of the lav open. Adam sat on the toilet inside, his pants down to his ankles. He was leaning back stroking his seven inch penis looking straight into Fred's eyes. Fred moved in and spun around to lock the door. Without a thought, Fred dropped to his knees and swallowed the soldier's cock, forcing the thick shaft all the way inside until the soft sandy hairs tickled his nose. His throat stretched to accommodate the thick mushroom head. He began to suck Adam's cock like a starving man, licking, slurping, stroking, and swallowing over and over. The young man's hands rested on Fred's head guiding his sucks and lifting his ass up off the john to drive his cock deeper and deeper into the man's mouth until he gagged with the thrusting. The soldier's precum flowed like maple sap into his mouth as he worked his cock with his mouth, stopping long enough to stuff as much of the soldier's balls into his mouth as he could fit, bathing them both with his tongue, letting thick drips of saliva slide down the smooth sack to the young man's hidden ass crack.

Suddenly, Adam moved forward, performing a magic contortion act that seemed impossible while Fred sat on the toilet, with the soldier's smooth, round ass hovering in front of his face. Fred grabbed the meaty ass and pulled the cheeks apart. The soft, light brown fuzz in the crack was smooth and almost golden. Fred pressed his face into the crack and licked down the crease until he found the young man's hole, dusty brown and soft. He pressed his tongue against it again and again until he penetrated the muscle. He pushed hard within until the pucker was wet and open with spit. Adam's hand pushed on the back of Fred's head, driving the man's face deeper and deeper into the soldier's ass. Adam's face turned around and stared at Fred. It was weak and filled with desire.

"Fuck me, Dad. Get your cock in me," he hissed softly.

He maneuvered around until his ass was the perfect height and angle. Fred stood and pushed his pants down to his ankles. His cock was ready to explode, rigid and leaking. He spat a glob of saliva onto the tip and let it find the soldier's manhole. It was hot and wet with his licking. He pushed forward and felt the muscle give up and the young man grunted softly as he slammed inside balls deep.

"Holy fuck, Dad. Breed me, man. Make me your bitch, buddy."

Fred fucked like a jackhammer: hard, deep and relentless. The small room filled with the scent of sweat and ass. The soldier gripped the counter and roof and pushed his ass deeper and deeper onto Fred's thick cock. Fred gripped Adam's hips and fucked in long strokes, the smacks of his belly and balls echoing in the room. The floor bucked and rocked, jostling the men as Fred plowed the young man's asshole. The seat belt sign illuminated in the lavatory.

"Breed me, now!" he commanded, then added, "Oh shit, I'm gonna cum."

A thick blast of white nut jetted from his penis and splashed on the mirror over the sink. He groaned and three more thick ropes plastered the mirror and sink. Fred drove his cock deep into the soldier's ass one last time and grunted low, seeding Adam's ass with thick white semen. Leaning his head and chest against the soldier's back, his breath hard and heavy. There was a soft knock on the door.

"Excuse me. You need to return to your seat. The captain has turned on the seat belt sign." Then in a lower voice. "Freddy, you boys need to be quiet and get out of there," Henry said.

Adam turned around with a wicked grin and pulled Fred into a long, deep kiss. "Way to go, Dad. You got us busted."

Fred's face went crimson. The men fumbled and pulled their pants back up and tucked in their shirts. Adam grabbed a wad of tissues and wiped off the mirror and the sink, but large smears remained. He looked back at Fred and unlocked the door and pushed it open. Henry stood outside wagging a finger back and forth.

"Really?" he whispered. Adam just smiled and shrugged. He left the lavatory quickly followed by a mortified Fred, his face still glowing bright red. The men scrambled to their back row and fell over one another back into their seats and buckled up. Henry stood in the door of the lav taking in the carnage of the haz mat left behind by the men. He waved his hand in front of his nose and turned back to glare at the men. "Oh my God," he mouthed in mock indignation. Fred wanted to vanish but Adam seemed to actually swell with pride.

"I've wanted to join the mile high club for a long time, Dad," Adam said. His hand slid inside Fred's thigh up high near the man's sack.

"I can't believe we just did that," Fred replied moving his hand to the fatigue covered muscled thigh beside him.

"I haven't ever been fucked that good, Dad. You dominated me like a pro. I've never cum like that without even touching my dick."

Fred smiled and leaned in close to the soldier. "I don't want this fucking flight to end," he whispered.

"Me either."

Fred slid his hand inside the soldier's big hand again. "Why in the hell are you being so great to me. Are you just that horny or..?"

Adam chuckled. "No doubt I am one big horn dog, but no, man. Like I said. I get way more turned on with a guy like you than someone like me. I mean, guys like me are cool and look great and like you said, I wouldn't kick them out of bed probably. But I want a guy who has his shit together. And one who knows how to fuck me like a real man. I'm not even a fucking bottom and I want to do that again like right now."

Fred squeezed his hand. "That was the best sex of my whole life, big guy."

Adam smiled but sighed and his face fell into a pensive stare at the back of the seat in front of him. Fred watched for a moment, sliding his fingers in between the soldier's.

"You okay, buddy?"

"Yeah. Just not looking forward to getting off and heading back home. You know? Not really wanting to face the drama with the fam. Hear all about how President Obama is going to take away everyone's guns and force all good white people to become Muslim. Not to mention the constant reminders I am going to hell if I don't repent of my sinner ways."

Fred gripped the young man's hand with his other. "Do you have any other place to go?"

"Nah. Need a job and all that now. It's kind of like turning back into a teenager, being all dependent on your folks."

The men sat in silence feeling the rock and jostling of the plane as it continued on through the turbulent night. Fred stroked the soldier's hand as he held it, feeling the young man's melancholy seep into his heart. A thought came to him. It was crazy, probably reckless. But he couldn't get rid of it. It bored into his mind like a canker worm. He leaned close to talk directly into Adam's ear.

"So just come home with me. There's room. I only have my boys' part of the time and they are pretty grown up anyway. It's about time they figured out why their mom and I split up. Shit, I think they might know already. I don't care. If you need a place for a while, you can stay with me. It would be the best thing ever. No pressure or anything. I'm not trying to make you my boyfriend or something. I just don't want you to go home to non-stop ball busting. It's not right after everything you've done for our country and all that."

Adam stared at Fred. His blue eyes filled with tears at the corners. "Why would you do that? You don't even know me."

Fred smiled. "Fuck me but I think I know you better than my own kids right now. I'm lonely, buddy. To have you around, even if it's just for a while, would fill up my heart."

"What if I don't ever want to leave? What if I want your big dick in my ass from now on - except for the times when I am balls deep in you?"

"That sounds like a dream come true. I figure you will shake off this dad phase before too long. Shit man, I have three boys remember. Not all that much younger than you."

"I've wanted little brothers for a long time."

Fred groaned. "I can just hear my ex talking about this." In a mocking shrewish voice he continued, "I always knew you were a perv, you've been wanting to fuck a boy for a long time. "

"Well she's right about that," Adam said with a laugh.

Fred looked deep into Adam's eyes. "I don't know what the future holds for me or for you. But I would love for you to be in it, however you want to be. Even if it's just a good friend who needs someone to talk to or a place to land once in a while."

"And if I wanted it to be even more?"

Fred shook his head. Tears stung his own eyes now. "It would be the greatest day of my life."

Adam leaned over and turned Fred's chin toward his face and kissed him deeply. For the first time in his life, Fred didn't care. When he looked up, no one was turned around except that damn high school boy from a few rows up. The kid looked at Fred and lifted his eyebrows and proceeded to slide his finger into his cupped hand in a fuck-you gesture. Fred shrugged and grinned, not giving a shit.

~~The End~~

Also by this Author:

The Hotshot Brotherhood

Brokeback Buddies

Drive My Engine, Rookie

South Patrol Pounding

Shower of Power

The Pardoned Series, Book 1 - Rise From Abyss

The Pardoned Series, Book 2 - Rescued

Wild Knights of Heat

Son Swap

Bad Sheriff

Here Comes Trouble

Fighting My Instincts

From the Author

WANT FREE COPIES OF MY BOOKS?
Just visit my blog and download free copies of my books:
http://angus-macgregor.awesomeauthors.org/angus-macgregor/

If you enjoyed any of my books then please share the love and click like on my books in Amazon. Your reviews are greatly appreciated.

One Last Thing, For Kindle Readers...

When you turn the page, Kindle will give you the opportunity to rate this book and share your thoughts on Facebook and Twitter. If you enjoyed my writings, would you please take a few seconds to let your friends know about it? Because... when they enjoy they will be grateful to you and so will I.

Thank You!

Angus MacGregor
angus_macgregor@awesomeauthors.org

About the Author

Angus MacGregor resides with his family in Oregon and Hawaii. Along with his passion for writing, Angus enjoys growing orchids, snorkeling and hiking.

Angus has worked as a school teacher, a financial analyst, and a small business developer. He currently works as a writer and supports firefighting efforts by working on wildfires in the US during the summer months. In addition to his adult erotica books, Angus has recently completed his first book of mainstream fiction.

"I love seeing what the Universe has in store for me as I create this reality. I love my life and the blessings of all the people and gifts that surround me. I wish peace and blessings to all my readers."

WANT FREE COPIES OF MY BOOKS?
Just visit my blog and download free copies of my books:
http://angus-macgregor.awesomeauthors.org/angus-macgregor/